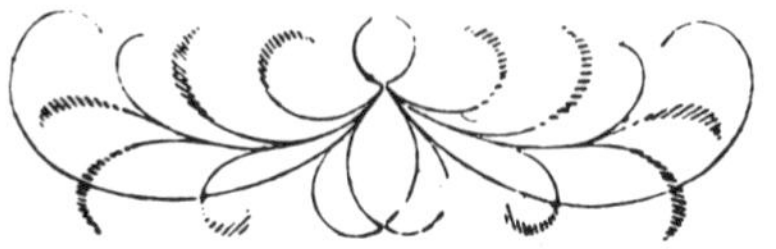

For Isabel, who was too small to be there

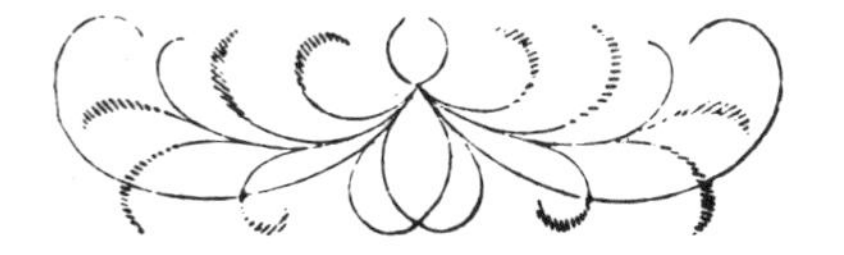

by Jane Yolen
with photographs by Gabriel Amadeus Cooney

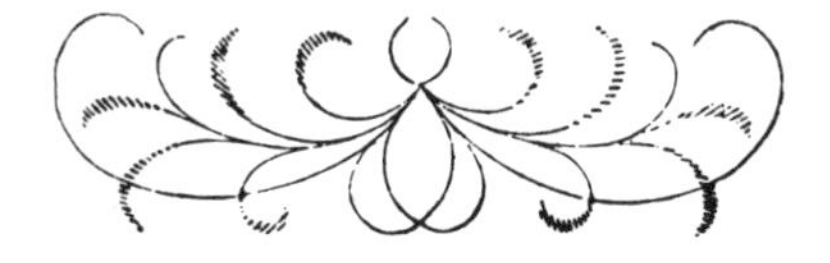

 Published simultaneously in Canada
by Fitzhenry & Whiteside Limited, Toronto.
Designed by Richard M. Ference
Manufactured in the United States of America

THOMAS Y. CROWELL COMPANY NEW YORK

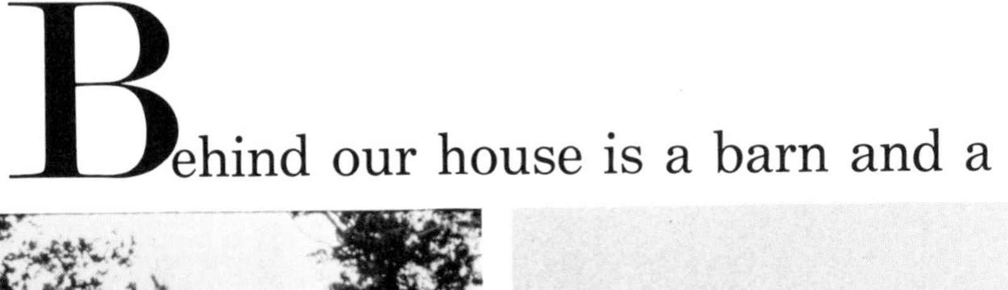
Behind our house is a barn and a

forest and a field of wildflowers and weeds. Mostly milkweeds.

Almost every summer day
my brother and sister and
I go down to the barn

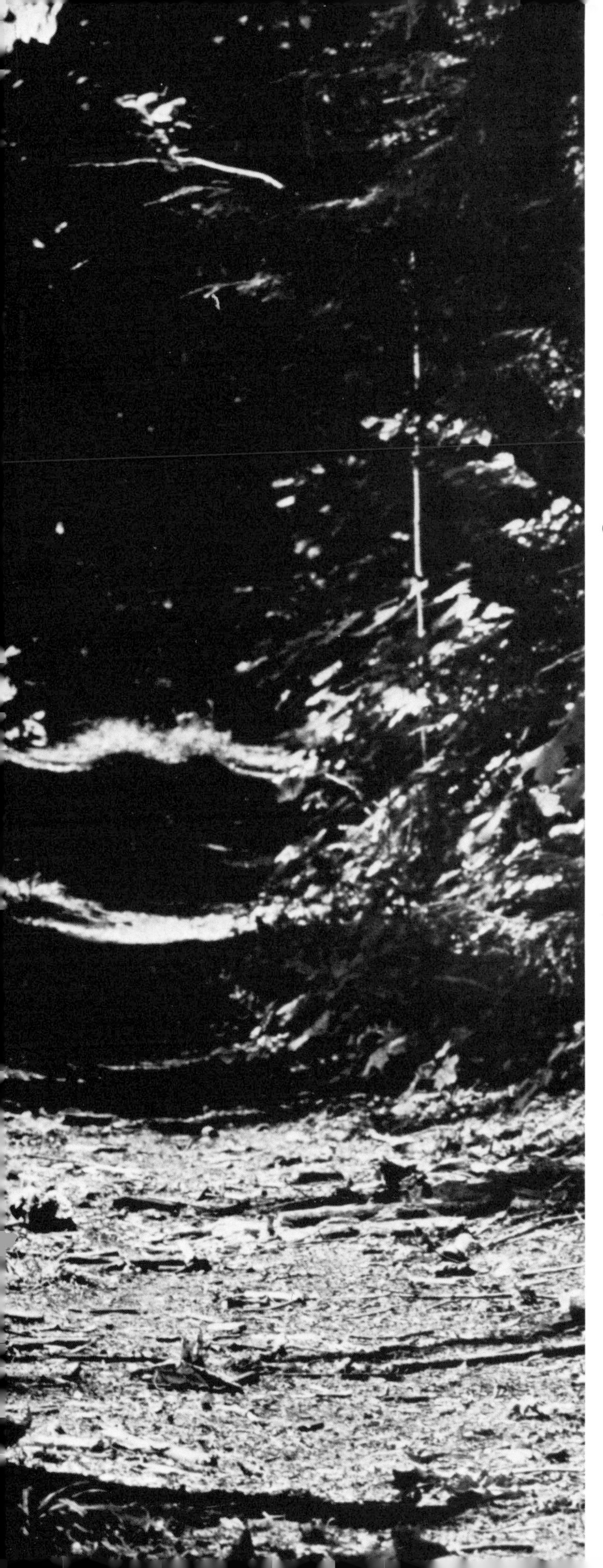

or run along the forest paths.

But we especially like to go up to the field where the milkweeds grow. The plants stand as high as my head. Only my sister is taller. Than me. Than the milkweeds. My little brother disappears in the milkweed wood.

A few weeks ago along the meadow way we could find Queen Anne's lace and sweet-smelling clover, king devil, bluets, and rye. And there were milkweed flowers in the field.

Now the milkweed flowers have changed. Like a prince turned into a frog. Bumpy and rough. But hiding a secret beautiful thing inside.

I know the secret. I know what beautiful thing is inside. It's just like me when I'm unhappy or mad. All bumpy and rough on the outside. Then Mommy says there's a secret beautiful Adam inside. Like a milkweed pod, she says. Holding. Waiting. Waiting to be set free.

Watch the pod burst open. There's the secret. Just like a cloud. Or like silk. Or September snow. It tickles my hand. It's soft on my cheek.

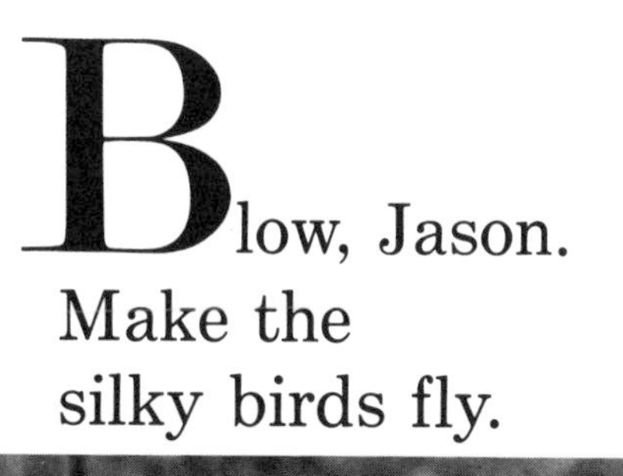

Blow, Jason.
Make the
silky birds fly.

Let's run. Let's catch them.

Catch and blow again.

Quick, an unopened
pod in my pocket.

I'll hold it against my
cheek when I go to bed, warm
under great-grandmama's
quilt. For all my winter dreams.
When I dream of the fields
full of sweet-smelling flowers;

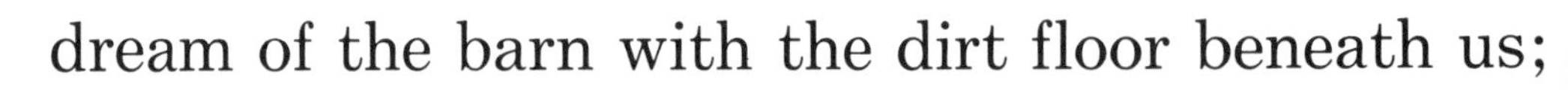

dream of the barn with the dirt floor beneath us;

dream of the forest with trees tall as towers;

dream of the
summer, dream of the
milkweed days.

Jane Yolen's published works include novels, poetry, picture books, biographies and other nonfiction, and short-story collections. They have brought her many awards, such as the Golden Kite Award of the Society of Children's Book Writers, won by *The Girl Who Cried Flowers,* which was also chosen by the American Library Association as a Notable Children's Book and was a runner-up for the National Book Award. Her books have been translated and published in Europe and in Asia, and she is widely known as a creator of original fantasies in the classic folktale tradition. A graduate of Smith College, she has been an editor and teacher as well as a writer.

The theme of *Milkweed Days* sprang from actual experience: Jane Yolen has had much opportunity to observe small children interacting with the world of nature, as she lives with her husband and their three children in a lovely old farmhouse, surrounded by woods and meadows, in Hatfield, Massachusetts.

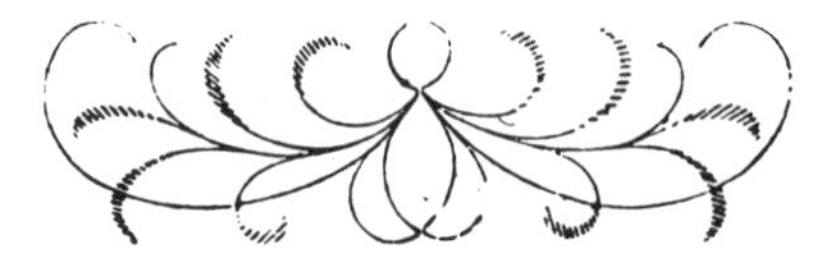

Gabriel Amadeus Cooney began his photographic career eleven years ago, with a Kodak Brownie camera on a trip to North Africa. He enjoys traveling and has worked for a film company in cities all over the United States. *Milkweed Days* is his first book for children. Some of the work from his most recent exhibition at Deerfield Academy has become a part of the collection at the Museum of Art, Smith College. Mr. Cooney, as a freelance photographer, has his own studio and lives in West Whately, Massachusetts, with his wife and his young daughter.

Library of Congress Cataloging in Publication Data

Yolen, Jane H. Milkweed days.
SUMMARY: A young boy uses a milkweed pod kept from the previous year to remind him of summer.
[1. Milkweed—Fiction. 2. Summer—Fiction]
I. Cooney, Gabriel Amadeus. II. Title.
PZ7.Y78Mg [E] 76-10273
ISBN 0-690-01250-0 ISBN 0-690-01140-7 (lib. bdg.)